Sofia
the First

The Floating Palace

ISBN 978-0-545-74387-7

12 11 10 9 8 7 6 5 4 3 2 1   14 15 16 17 18 19/0

Printed in the U.S.A.

First Scholastic printing, April 2014

40

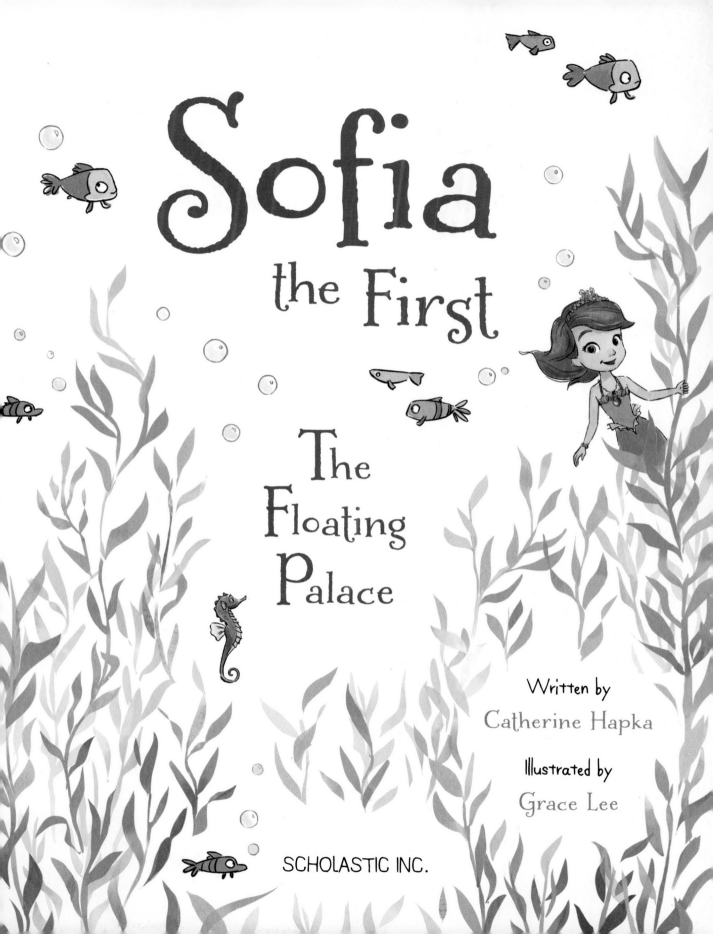

Sofia
the First

The Floating Palace

Written by
Catherine Hapka

Illustrated by
Grace Lee

SCHOLASTIC INC.

I'm Sofia

and I love being a

princess.

For our summer vacation, my family is visiting Merroway Cove on our boat.

It's so big it's more like a floating palace!

Lately, I've been reading about mermaids.
Maybe we'll see one at the cove. I hope so!
But Dad says mermaids aren't real.

My dad, King Roland, is usually right about most things—but he's wrong about mermaids.

Because when I go onto the deck of our floating palace, there she is—a real, live mermaid!

"Help!" the mermaid cries.
Oh, no! She's tangled in a net!

"Let me help you," I say. I pull her onto
the boat and help untangle her.
"Thank you!" she says. Her name is Oona.
She's really nice. But then she says she has to go.

"We're not supposed to spend time above the water,"
she explains. But when Oona gets in the water,
she can't swim. Her fin is hurt.

As I slide into the water to help her,
my amulet glows—and I turn into a

mermaid!

I can't believe it!
And neither can Oona.
"How did you do that?" Oona asks.
I tell her about my **magical amulet.**
Oona has a comb that's enchanted, too.
"I'm not sure what its powers are,"
says Oona. "But Mom says she'll
tell me when I'm older."

I help Oona swim toward her home in the cove. We swim past a kelp forest, a cool sunken ship, and hundreds of beautiful fish.

When we get near Oona's home, I meet
her friend, Sven the seahorse, and her big sister, Cora.
They use moon kelp to heal Oona's tail.

Suddenly, the water goes dark.
It's our floating palace
stopping above us.

Then we hear Oona's mom
calling her and Cora home.
Oona's mom is the
mermaid queen.

"I'm so glad you're safe!" she exclaims. "A human vessel is in the cove, and humans are dangerous."

But I'm not dangerous, and neither is my family. Queen Emmaline doesn't know that, though.

And she wants to use her magic trident to create a powerful storm—one that could blow the floating palace out of the cove, or maybe even sink it! My family is on that ship!

So I tell the queen that
I'm a human and I can get the ship to leave.
"Please don't sink it. Just give me a chance," I say.
Luckily, the queen agrees to let me try.
Oona and Cora wish me luck.

I start swimming back to the floating palace.
Suddenly, I hear Oona calling my name.

Oh, no! A horrible, hideous sea monster is
chasing her! He wants her enchanted comb.
I swim after them as fast as I can, but
then they enter the kelp forest.

"Oona!" I cry.
There's no answer.

I rush back to tell Queen Emmaline what happened, and she tells me I have till sundown to rescue Oona.

The queen says if I can't, she'll sink the floating palace!

I swim back to the floating palace. I need help. But my family **doesn't believe** in mermaids.

So I gather some friends who **do believe**—Sven, Clover, and a seagull named Farley.

Finally, we find Oona. The sea monster
has her trapped and he's about to steal her
enchanted comb. I try to stop him, but he's very
powerful—he almost captures me, too!

Oh, no!

Queen Emmaline is starting loud thunder over the cove!
I need to rescue Oona before her mom sinks my family's ship.
I don't know what to do. . . .

"Uh, your necklace is glowing," Sven tells me.

When we dive underwater,
Princess Ariel appears!
My amulet brought her to help.
So I tell Ariel about Oona.
"I tried to save her, but . . ."
"You need more help," Ariel says.
She tells me that humans and
mermaids both love their families,
and if we just work together . . .

Now I know what to do!

Sven and I find
Cora and tell her
about the sea monster.

"He's after Oona's comb,"
I explain. "The only
way to save her is for us
to work together."

So Cora and I
come up with a plan.
Sven, Farley, and Clover help, too.

I have to sneak onto the boat where the sea
monster has Oona trapped. I get there just
as he is about to cast a spell to grab Oona's
comb. But I snatch it right out of his hand!

"Give me the comb and I'll let your mermaid friend go," the sea monster says.

"What if I don't?" I say.

"Then I'll cast a spell on you and make you disappear!"

I step in front of Oona's
cage. Then I toss the comb
overboard where Cora is
waiting to catch it.

"No you don't!"
the sea monster howls.
He flicks his wand at me . . .

but I jump out of the way.
Instead of making **me**
disappear, he makes Oona's
cage vanish!

Oona is free! But the sea monster is **furious**. He points his wand at us.

"You won't trick me again!" he warns.

Suddenly, Farley flies
over the sea monster—
and **drops** Clover
right on top of him!

Then Farley **swoops** down
and grabs his wand.

Cora holds up the comb
as it starts to **glow!** "Waters,
rise at my command!" she cries.
Then a spiral of water blasts the
sea monster across the cove!

We rush back to Queen Emmaline.
"Thank goodness you're safe!" the queen cries.
She raises her trident to stop the storm.
Whew! Now my family is safe, too!

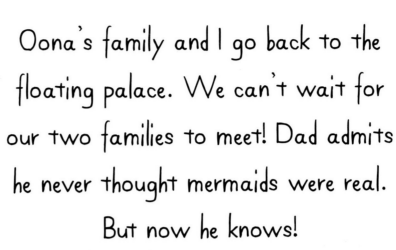

Oona's family and I go back to the
floating palace. We can't wait for
our two families to meet! Dad admits
he never thought mermaids were real.
But now he knows!

I sit with Oona and watch the sun set.
She's a mermaid, and I'm a human.
But I know

we'll be friends forever!

The End